THRUST

Also by Heather Derr-Smith

Tongue Screw
The Bride Minaret
Each End of the World

THRUST

POEMS

HEATHER DERR-SMITH

A Karen & Michael Braziller Book
PERSEA BOOKS /NEW YORK

Persea Books, Inc.
277 Broadway
New York, New York 10007

Library of Congress Cataloging-in-Publication Data
Names: Derr-Smith, Heather, author.
Title: Thrust : poems / Heather Derr-Smith.
Description: New York : Persea Books, 2017. | "A Karen & Michael Braziller book."
Identifiers: LCCN 2016058560 | ISBN 9780892554867 (original trade pbk. : acid-free paper)
Classification: LCC PS3604.E7546 A6 2017 | DDC 811/.6—dc23
LC record available at https://lccn.loc.gov/2016058560

Book design and composition by Rita Lascaro
Typeset in Minion
Manufactured in the United States of America. Printed on acid-free paper.

Contents

*

"Make a law that loves the one who breaks it."
—LARRY LEVIS

"Satan visibly and palpably raignes in Virginia, more
than any other known place in the world."
—WILLIAM CRASHAW, 1613

THRUST

Hide Out

Briefest reflection
                                two children's faces in the spring,
a brother and a sister with filament hair, and beyond their heads,

a house on the hill, all of it battlefield. These two go at it
               every day, shoveling the red dirt out and roofing it with plywood,

resourceful, army canteens and hatchets hooked to their belts,
                     nails between their teeth. Oh, how he protected her,

how he stood against their father when he freighted down the long hall,
                  oh how he bent his head like a shield while she cowered.

Now in the pit they've tunneled, in the house they've rooted out,
                he digs his fingers in her. He's strong,

made for coming like a second coming. She's
                 made for taking it, taking all of the earth into her body.

In a year, her brother runs away across the country
                     back to Texas, no more war.

Back at the house, the walls ache. The doors of the rooms
barred shut. Their father's footsteps rattle the threshold, shotguns

leaning against the bedframe, loaded and cocked.

She still snuck into the woods at night after her brother had gone
                   to the covering their own hands built,

where they once leaned against each other in the dark, the whippoorwill's
                                          song
balled and trilling in the fists of their hearts.

Glass Jaw

Stand there at the lip of the pit, *girl,* slabs of concrete and *weep holes,*
                    your daddy called them. Eleven then and this house

would be your first house built for a purpose, the dream
            of your mother assembled out of her desperate and split lives,

split lips after the fight, blood like a craving on your chin.

The house would make it right, pine beams mapping out a new territory of sane.

The house was built on Twin Springs,
                    subterranean creeks running through abandoned mines,

fault lines gathered on the topography like ruffles
            on a child's skirt. The shrink and swell clays sparkled with gold,

fool's gold. I see you, hunched over the dirt to gather it up, collect
            its promises in your gingham apron,
            smocking pockets bloomed with blue smoke.

The past is connected to the present *like a man's arm to his shoulder,*

the punch that breaks the jaw in pieces, the hit that leaves you speechless.

Hazel Run

I just entered you, he said. Like name it and claim it.
                          The preacher on the radio winds his black stole
                          around your eyes. Small red clots of

language between my legs. This is where the girl was found. Hot Tramp.

Down at the creek, carrying so much blood during the Battle of Wilderness,

the swollen banks burst. The children knew this history by instinct,
                          war between brothers. Your body

just obeyed, crouch and clinch, the reflex against another body

in its strike.

Before the violence of adulthood was the violence of childhood
and before that a whole history of bloodshed as inheritance.

We waded in the shallow waters, the flash and stab of pyrite
                and sunlight and the strike of the flint in our hands, all of it

exploded ordnance, tracers of bullets to mark a place
                    deeply as only war does.

We were always injured down there in our woods, in the waters of our creek,
ankles serrated, braceleted in barbed wire, our fingers stippled

from the pincers of the crawdads we caught and released,
                    drops of our cells like blotches of ink on the wet pebbles,

seeping into the sparkling sand. I went back and mapped it out

with GPS. Nothing had changed. Same dogwoods, same groove of trench and
                                mounds,
the ghosts of us, still barefoot in the water,

same breath-hold break-point, same drown.

Catherine's Furnace

There were diamonds in the ground beneath us
         formed out of the volcanic rock, hidden in the smelting mines.
We could feel them, pulsing, pinging like radar into our prayers.

Ours was a family of seekers, pick ax and lust, searching
         for a substitution, some bread and wine for what was lost.

My mother's Jesus and Reagan, my stepfather's beer and secretaries,
their joint quest of catharsis in lusts and fistfights, headbutt and pulled hair,
the sawdust trail of the tent revival.

I know one thing.
I was worth beating down, a pulp. Someone *wanted* me so damn bad,
like a desire that was desperate, hogtied.
Didn't it feel like some kind of love, *baby girl*, rabbit-punched?

I found out years later, my real father hunted butterflies,
like Nabokov, the blue ones, all over North America,
aerial net in his delicate hands,
cabinets of fastened apex, thorax pinched between thumb and forefinger,
scent of napthalene.

He would spend days lost in the Paris Museum, drawers sliding open and
                                        shut,
rustle of pearl-bordered forewings and blue crenuled hind wings,
tiny scales on his fingers and palms in lustrous dust.

I imagined them coming in waves to the New World.

I didn't know who my father was; he'd just gone one day
when I was very young, a throbbing in my neck, cervical vertebra burst.

Under the seraph's beat, a deflagration of the self, burning away to suck it all in,
something never there from the beginning, irretrievable

as the dead, lingering, the way the dead do in resistance,
like the ticks we burned with a match. Or the startle
of recognition when the mockingbird sings and flies away
and then you grow weary with the song and come to know

it was just an imitation of some other beast.

What you thought was there, substantial,
was just the wind's thickly veined limbs in the false indigo.

Nabokov said nature was a form of magic, like art.

The grub-bored holes in the moth's wings, imitating a leaf,
enchantment and deception, he said.

My home was No Man's Land, perfume of magnolias in the dusk.
The prophet said, *Put hot coals on your head.*

Make love out of the kick and the punch.
Make beauty out of cunt, a glowing ember.

The Quarry

The cliffs rose fifty feet above the clear water,
               and nestled at the bottom, fifty feet below,
were the caverns of sunken school buses.
               Inside the hull the high school girls peeled off their underwear,
floating balloons of their sex, hair between their legs
               like rapid-coils of a bomb in the current.

From the cliffs, the boys leapt into the sky, their voices ricocheted
               and clapped against the stone in a clatter of wingbeats,
frenzied flight as they fell, or were they flying?
               Those boys, half-naked
in the sunlight were like gods, are like gods now. I watch them at this distance,
               their feints and side-steps
and hooks as they sparred, bare feet on the warm rock.
               Some of them would still want to fuck,
but what I liked is how they seemed to me oblivious to their sex
               in a way that girls weren't allowed to be. The boys were bodies
of pure delight, a buzzing heat in the fiber and chord
               of their nerves that I was barred from. No dichotomy in them,
more than lust, an inhabitation that is perfectly at home
               in its leap and thrust.
At fifteen I wanted to be them. I want to be them now.
               The boy of myself, leaping over the edge.
I watch them plunge down
               and then rise like a bullet,
breaking back up into air, breathless as methamphetamine,
               a rush of wind in the magnolias, in the locusts,
racines of white flowers and fragrance, the boys, the boys
               swinging like a pendulum in the blooms
back to the beginning, the source
               of abandonment, their laughing, flung joy.
Stepping into the boyhood of my girlhood
               a double barreled shotgun of myself, and shot.
I said I could stiffen you in two seconds
               and he said, *Stiffen this.*

I-95

Rain handwritten in the leaves of the silverbell, their white trumpets,
slips of ghosts in the dark drawing in fast at my back.
                        Here I am in the inner courtyard, your face like a slap.

René Char said, bring the ship nearer to its longing.
                                    Well, I keep trying,
sneaking out the windows at seventeen and throwing myself
                        from airplanes over the devouring seas. It's no use,
like a ouija board, I keep turning back up
in the place where it all began, an ideomotor effect of the fingers in the mind,
                        labia parted like specimen, like snarl.

The lights of the interstate sweep with wings. Oh, Otherworld, I hear your
                                                            chatter.
                        I followed the edge of the highway, keeping low,
esophageal tunnel of woods, *hush, hush*

and I sang the whole way north and every song was a psalm to you,
                        the you of my future lover, the you of arrival and advent,

the you that sprang from my guts every time I was hit or kicked,
                        green bruises like the leaves in the boughs.
The you of my being I imagined beautiful out of the penetralia
of that molt self. Promiscuous with love,

its viscera in the cup of my mouth. Brake lights of cars like hibiscus
                        against the black umbilical road, a house left behind, cut off.

The cunnilingual softness of night closing in, head thrown back.

Stitch

She shrugged and slipped out of her yellow dress, the garments of love
$$\text{dropping off,}$$
and went into the woods.

Spiders the shape of jewels
$$\text{crept around her naked body. Bluebirds}$$
rasped their prayers in the crowns of the Virginia pines.

In the house of her childhood, now empty,
$$\text{rage like chain-lightning threw its fists,}$$

the count in seconds quivering against her pubis. She outlasted them all,
her own cloud of witness. She rubbed her language against the skin of theirs,

the sobbing in the closet behind the silk nightgowns
and the AR-15's,
$$\text{a force that had seemed unstoppable, nitroglycerin in her veins,}$$

threatening to blow them all to smithereens. She was untouchable,
outside of the reach of God, *Heathen.*

In the end, they had all been frightened of her, how she rose from the blows,
like the ring of a bell, unbreakable.

Performed pain is still pain

That girl, too needy, no
not needy, giving everything.
$$\text{Hit the rock with the staff, the gush—}$$

Out of her swollen throat, crazy, derelict, groan.

By you, she means looking directly at her.

So she's hit again. Hit once. Hit again when she ducks.
$$\text{So her dad kicks her down the hall.}$$

The toppled X on Golgotha hung on its nail on the living room wall.

It's OK, going to be OK, she whispered to the stranger's neck
as he pinned her against the bed.

She sang the *Liebeslied.*
She is *shhh, shhh* soothing him.

Her self a moon, a moan,
mounds of stars.

Blur of wings in the larches.
Ring of desire around her neck, torquated.
She's sailing around your lamp like a moth, the singe on the edge of herself.

It's not even a voice she asked for,
but little scratches in the dust of words is all.

Flash

Above the dinner table hung one of those stained glass lamps
that used to hang in the Pizza Hut, imitation Tiffany.

It seemed to me as a child
to be a light of some imminent celebration, a portent
for an occasion of love.
                    To own a lamp like that was a promise,
a reward, meant that on this night,
around supper, someone might take a portrait of us gathered
as proof that we had been happy.
                    The light tipped,
spilled sanguineous on the linoleum tiles,
bathing the beige carpet blood red as the lamp swung on its chain,
and I can see my mother's back
turned against us and my stepfather's face closing in.
Wave your red flags, sharpen your spears.

It was all Coney Island then, the organ music speeding up,
                    screams from the roller coasters.
Jeanie the Living Half-Girl.
The Only One in the World. Step right up and see
                    the strong man with his mallet.

My brother and I hid under the table, listening for the hit.
Her satin blouse, a luminous fire.
The vein in his neck popped and bulged like an erection.

In a flash

we are struck, a ruined photograph, fogged by the accident
of exposure.
                    A trap door slides open and my brother's hands dissipate,
my mother's nostrils bleed in wisps like red hair, and my stepfather's face
                                        ignites

and then we all snuff out.

K.O.

The fog fingered along the cemetery wall
where the Confederate dead lay buried

and where we used to walk, my mother
and me, her stories of ghosts, stories of loss.

She pushed me against the ground, knees in the grass,
kicked me, screaming, when I told her

my secret, that I'd had sex with a boy,

and she wailed, *But he's ugly! He's ugly!*
as I knelt beneath the statue of the unknown soldier.

Her hands tightened their ligaments
around my neck. I can't say the word, on the tip

of my tongue. Always a slip, a half-rhyme.
I wrote her letters, said she was *love,*
meaning ligature.

Her beautiful blue eyes, violent stars.
Her words fast as bullets or copperhead strike.

Infighting and outfighting,
sally and punch with your right,

Punch with your right.   I forgive you.

She says, *Yesterday I was lying, but today
I am telling the truth.*

I believe you.

Blood tattooing her silk robe.

Blood like the shaped-notes of an old hymn dripping from her mouth.

O could she sing. I can hear her now,
so many years later,
His Eye is on the Sparrow, ringing through the live oaks.

Her beautiful voice, rising suddenly from my own throat,
surprise. It's too late, explosion of stars.
Left hook.

Gouge

One man said *there are hundreds*
of delicate articulated bones
in the human head. So don't
get punched. Easier said than done.
You see his risen fist, her lowered neck.
See the blank canvas sails of God's back
and the river hemorrhaging
the past, spheres of blood in free fall,
and the splatter you can read like a map,
fingers tracing the convergences.
On the road ahead, there's a dead end,
and no one to portage with.
But I'll find my way, she said,
to no one in particular, no one left.
It'll be all right, she said, running away.
It's going to be OK, she said, her hands
on the back of the man who raped her.
Oh Rappahannock, Oh all you drowned girls.
Jack in the pulpit burst from the seams,
and the trout lily was up,
meaning it was time to fish. *Shhh, quiet now,*
little brother crying over the hooked lip.
Watch her go, lights flash, starboard and port.
Look, the girl's frail arms like bones
lift the boat. The starlight on the water
twinkling of eyes. Thief in the night.
She's Nancy Drew hiding out in a cove.
She's got it all plotted out,
location by sectioning, or *Where am I?*
The place where the bearing lines cross.
Look, the girl's hands turn to oars
and there she goes
far beyond the skies.

XXX

The ventricles of the bush, thorns, & orchids
burst their arteries in the woods.

Rhododendrons, thrush in liturgy & lyric.

The girl was phantasmagorical, huge, oracle.
No common thing, not yours, not belonging to you.

She sang like Jeanne Moreau, the Tourbillon,
wore bells on her ankles. The boys loved her,

but they were scared of her, too, walking down there
in the woods behind the Home for Troubled.

They knew what was what and what was wrong, sin
from the get-go, the centerfold of *Nugget* magazine.

One boy pushed her down in the honeysuckle
and tried to fuck her, but she punched him off, jab

to the neck, her palm facing the ground. In an instant
he turned blue, irridescent as an ejaculation of feathers

in the shimmering light. The insects buzzed from auricle
to chambers deep and sucking. The girl's hair lifted like veins—

not biblical, not evangelical, but something primitive
and voodoo. Made of stardust. Made of dirt.

Made of slut.

Last Breath

Listening to "Please Mr. Gravedigger" on your

bed

and here is a photograph of us kissing.

Tripping on mushrooms and the Civil War dead come up out of the road
and the man we picked up hitchhiking

led us down the backway and said, *I've got a cow up in that barn I'm just
fixin' to fuck. Y'all wanna come?* and we said no thank you

in all Southern politeness and backed the car out, gravel spitting like a
speckled bird. I vomited the rest of the night

in Buddy's bathroom, walls plastered with pornography.
You wrapped me in an afghan on the couch and pressed your fingers

to my forehead, saying it was magic and I'd be made well.

Your family was lost to you and mine roams the town
trying to catch me up in their claws. Fredericksburg, Virginia,

humid morning light the color of piss in the magnolias, ghosts hanging
from the balconies and bell towers.

Brother, lover, friend. Repeat. Brother, lover, friend.
My arithmetic. Insurgent and fugitive girl made infinite.

Girls, Guard Your Hearts, Cover Your Heads

Clouds snagged in the hooks of tree limbs,
Little Shepherd Trail and Shorty's got his shotgun in his lap

to kill the copperheads. The dogwoods
glow in the porch light. Rattle in the cherry orchard,

rattle in the well. A stranger in his plain Mennonite coat
                              pressed a pink paper tract against my palm,

Why Christian women wear the headship veiling

and I pressed back. Oh I pressed back. Shenandoah,

on an evening walk behind my brother's house, twilight like blue milk in
                                                            our hair,

our feet tracing the hidden fault line, no one knew was there until it shook.

            I held his daughter's hand in mine, and a coyote crossed our path

so large, it caught our breath: The kind that long ago
                      mated with wolves and grew to the size of a myth.

We sang a hymn of awe from our shut mouths as it passed and it stopped
and looked straight into us
                      with its yellow orbits of eyes.
                      Fur the color of flint, quivering over its ribs

and the shunting of its hooves in the red dust
                      speckled with the berries we spilled like blood in our surprise.
And I remembered the touch of his hand

and in the unfinished rooms of the dark
we heard a moan of love
                      between the legs of neither woman nor man.

To Keep Alive With You

I came back to Virginia to dig up what was lost

                                                     out of the vomit-scented clay.
The one beaten by police out at the farm,
blood in the vessels of your eyes, scatter shot.

There was the one who wrecked his father's DeLorean
                        and never went home again, just kept driving.

And the one I gave head in the Episcopal Church,
                      in George Washington's pew, wiping my lips
                      with a Jesus Built my Hotrod t-shirt.

                    We all wanted something so exquisite back then,
                      though at fifteen we were also greedy, ruthless in the world,
and like the ghosts that get sucked
                    into the thick stone walls and appear at will
                    running down the hall, drunk as hell, beating on the door,

when I went back, I found the core of what once was still flickering.

The guitarist's black-painted fingernails,
cannonballs embedded in the graveyard steps,
fringe of the fritillary perched on the wrought iron, bloodstains on the
                                        floorboards.

Now, I say, *Press yourself against me hard and crush my bones.*
Pull out my hair.

Drag me by the wrist in another direction,

to the Armory dance's mosh pit
or the old mill beside the Rappahannock where we laid our bodies in the
                                        sun, root hairs

lifting to touch the light.

Are you really gone, or never was?

A shade—under the willows, the water's stigmata in the rock.

I unbutton your summer shirt,
gold and green June bugs, scarabs
          with legs like hooks against your unloosing chest.

Sun goes down in the fretwork of trees.
The curtain draws over your face, body ached and open,
                      absolute stillness like a Eucharist.

*

St. Mark's in the Bouwerie Towers

The train I ride, sixteen coaches long. Elvis stamp in the corner of the postcard.
You're on the bus back to Brooklyn from a wedding in a barn.

I am not seducing you, I write back.

Here in Virginia
                    the monarchs are migrating
and I mistake their congregation
                    for a maple tree flaring its fires, the milkweed's ghost-like leaves

now transubstantiated into wings.

From three hundred miles away, I was this awestruck thing at the steps
of your pelvis,
                    or myself, a membrane you could lancinate,
hymen of an eye. I give you
                    the macula, that small pit of vision
that turns the color of flame after death,
                    a color never seen there in life.

This is the architecture of my longing,
sketched out in graphite pencil and ink on paper.

                    I write to you about the barn dance at my own wedding
on the Wilderness Battlefield, when a stranger met me down the line
and hooked my hip to the bone of his hip
                    and swung me so hard
                              my feet lifted from the ground.

I'm listening to the Passion of St. Mark, the lost one,
the passion they had to reconstruct.   *Thy body with her oils*

Here's your letter and mine, correspondences.
Your name at the beginning, my name at the end. And in between the long
                                                            waiting,
some kind of wordless dance between the words.

Montaigne said we can never really know another.
Isn't it better to just love?
Here's the lashed and hogtied want when I write, *Dear.*

Thank you for the postcard.

I won't let you vanish.

I'll write you back. I'll write you down.

I Come to the Garden Alone

A goldfinch bursts on the sunflower stalk, flame and scintillate.

The sunflower stalk does not believe any creature lives in the moment,

the moment says there is no moment,

just a coming and going, the body longing to touch and be touched.

The etch of our claws, scratching in the dust

some message the scripture left out of the canon,

invisible word we have to augur for ourselves,
                                    fingering the entrails.
Footprints like feather stitch in the dirt,

fern stitches, cross stitches, and arrowheads in my skin,
                                    little artifacts of origin and oracle.
Meet me at the end, True Love,

at the crossroads and coordinate of your body
                            and my body in its collision.

The flock startles and splits in sudden flight,

constellation of splatter on the wall of the room of us.

The cat sits at the window chattering her jaws with a bloodthirsty joy.

Stranger

My eyes ouija in his direction, he's next.
I'll keep you in the back of my closet with the petrol bombs.

He was a boy back from the Troubles,
smudge of bruises up his arms, red eyes like two raw abrasions.

In our neighborhood there were still ruins from World War II
and everywhere the men and women wore poppies in their lapels,

I could feel the accumulative weight of every action,
every sin an adhesion on your flesh and mine,

sound of piston and bolt in the night.

We took a drive to Northern England and saw the graves
carved with hollows in the shape of human bodies.

And in a cathedral, the waxen mold of an emaciated corpse
on top of the marble tomb. Our mother tongue,

this violence, just rediscovered. Some primitive language
we shared. He said he was going to marry me, didn't ask,

grabbed a handful of my hair, wound it around his wrists,
dragged me to his room in Camden Markets.

· · · · · ·

Black out under a new moon.
Hawkweed, gorse, and broom susurrate, slip the stitches

of their roots into the earth. The sound of their tips like the shutter
of film in the camera's slip and click. Maryon Park

at night, at the scene of the movie, scene of the crime,
in the spot where the man was shot, the outline of him shifts

and vanishes. I walk a little deeper in, trying to shove off the fear
of being caught. If you're not guilty, why are you running?

Sunrise like blood over the lintel. I keep running from the past.
I wonder what ever happened to him, and if he tried to track me down.

I can feel the wind follow like a tender ghost over the grasses, spangled
with moths and the acapella of crickets along the barrier wall of the Thames

as I ran on in the dark. When Wycliff wrote about the rapture he called it
rushed, as if all the saints would turn to water or wind. The image

of that soldier's face drifts like silk in the river, discarnate, and nameless now,
forgotten, he meant so little to me then. But looking back

I remember the bruises on his arms and I can feel his hair
under my hands. I remember the *body* of him.

* * *

It's Christmas and you wear a Santa hat, sweatshirt stained with blood.
Just a performance, fog machine behind the drumset, *I'm just pretending*

to be myself, you said. The look on your face, a killing jar, the mimicry
of the predator's eyes in the moth's giant wings. I've seen your girlish

and freckled hands smoothing the sheets in a photograph you took of the cat.
Everything about you is one step removed from my sight, a glimpse.

In the book you gave me, Nabokov cast an acetylene lamp over a white sheet
laid out on the grass on a moonless night, to catch some rare moths, a longing

he had, and it was the same lamp he would shine on Tamara, six years later.
He wanted us to know the moment. He wanted us to remember that moment
forever.

We will always be two strangers, always estranged.
Even Nabokov would come to know this, the last time

he saw her. She was walking away from him, hair and face wet from the rain.

Julian Schnabel in His Studio on West 111th Street

You wrote, *Out my window now I see morning rain*
and some old shoes tied to a fire escape.

That was the first day. A year later and the rain
falls outside my own Brooklyn room,

and the mourning doves murmured their songs
in the pocket of my ear. All of a sudden I woke up

and it was a new century and glass condos were rising
where the moon once cradled next to Venus

out on the prairie. Achromatic winter light. Julian Schnabel
lounging on a couch in his pajamas, a state of undressing,

but this is just a photograph,

the trace of light on a lens.
And these are just words, the trace of your hand.

In the postcard I write back to you

I am pressing my hand to your chest. I am touching you, full stop.

* * *

There is a river flowing beneath a foreign city, where I was young and still am
illuminated by lights in an underground tunnel.

You could drop your love-letters there in the cold stone water

and watch them float away like small boats.
Someone left a euphonium submerged—the water murmurs, it murmurs still,

trips over the valves and tubes, mouthpieces and bells
into the throat of a hidden song.

Not being able to touch is sometimes as interesting as touching

We are like these two stone cairns

set apart in separate seas, the waves breaking us down,
disappearing in the sand, uninhabitable.

And I'm some question you refuse to answer.

When I finally look in your eyes, I see your gaze
carding through my skin with its teeth,
like a comb in the lamb's fleece.
You bend down before you go and kiss me.

Does it exist between our bodies, do you feel it there in the dark,
some unknowable thing? We're not naked,
but there's a nakedness between us.

Listen, you can hear
the sound of my breath caught like wing beats against your neck

and the hawkmoths and the hummingbird moths in the dark,

tonguing the corolla.

Mercy Seat

River at night, carbon black, half-open door, a valve.
The fountains of the great deep burst apart.

When the rib was cut from Adam he was
separated from himself and hardly knew the loss

until he met it face to face.
I hope our correspondence gives you some relief.

I was raped, just a few years ago. He entered through the doorway,
pushed me into the room. I comforted him, spoke

to him like a mother to her son.

And that's the crux. Sometimes a stranger rips you apart
calls you a bitch and cunt and you say to him—

Do you know what you say? You say: *It's going to be OK.*
Everything is going to be all right.

Other times you want to put your hand in a stranger's torn side
and follow him across the threshold, through the opened door.

I've got a mandible, I've got a fibula with a greenstick fracture.
It hurts like lightning when it happens, your first touch.
It hurts with cold precision like a key slipping into its lock when you look at
me like that.

The Psalmist says, *All my bones should say who is like you.*

Insurgent

The woman levitated over Barcelona.
She had a rifle for a clavicle.
Her eyes were two black star dogs
bruising up the light.

She'll find you out, by hook or by crook,
tracing your fate with her fingers.

Shirt sleeves rolled up to the elbows,
she could climb the slope of the ridge,
gripping the roots. She could put
her own bloody hands

on your face and you would let her,
whiskers pricking under the heart-lines of her palms
like it's what you wanted all along.

The Sweet Spot

I go right up to you,
put my fingers in your mouth,
like I'm the woman in Goya,
fondling for the dead man's teeth.

Here comes the harsh morning light,
all night cutting
my thighs with a steak knife, half-berzerk
with desire for the ghost of you gone,
alcohol in the blood,
stinging as it seeps through the slit.

One man said to me look at that piece of ass.
I said watch out, my hands are slick and dry sticky.
No need to be scared, *Bang,* boy.
I've got you, won't let go.

This is the song of the sword
In the book of the wars of the Lord.

You said, when you throw a punch
don't aim for his face,
pick a spot behind his brain.

Zugenruhe

You're a small boy
down a thirty foot hole,
tremoring in the pit like a larynx.

While out on the Hudson river,
above the cold waters,
snow geese abound, shivering the
extravagant mouths of their sex.

Sometimes you're the whip
and I'm the skin on your thigh.
Sometimes I am the whip
easing between your legs.

Reclaim the body, its pain
even, ours to thrill and tremble.

A little bit of cut,
a little bit of blood. *Trust me.*

What we imagine like this together
is not an escape, but an insistence.

I needed to move on, see the meteorite
fall in the Mennonite farmer's field,
see its flash of lights against the silos—

The rose in his wife's garden cardiac and throbbing.

Give an account of this life,
size it up, impossible by impossible,
maybe just reach some kind of accord.

Gelassenheit is its opposite.
Time to get going.
Friend, accompany me.

The Virginia Museum of the Confederacy

Branches of live oak corkscrew into the blue sky.
Marsh bank addled and rotten.

What in nature is adamant? What insists of us?
The adamantine stone, fossils bearing witness
                      to time's dissolution of matter. This moment exists,
what are you going to do with it? Gone already.
                                The twinkling of an eye.
I was adamant, persistent. I crossed every boundary.
I did everything wrong.

The morning before I met you,
                    a homeless man followed me down the street
saying, *Come here you cunt. I'm going to kill you.*

                    But when you asked me how I was,
I said *good*, like God in the beginning declaring all things good.

You were eating your breakfast, hand covering your mouth.
I didn't know you,
            it was a chance encounter and I fell in love, all of a sudden,
yes, like a *shot*, like *trigger*.

On the stage in the bar, you lunged as you sang.
Seizure of starlings in the darkened Virginia sky, away from danger
in a sudden thrust of beauty.

Bludgeon of a storm coming in, bloodworm dangling
                  from its open mouth. And then the fragrance
of magnolias drips from the wet petals into my open hands.

I am unregenerate.
I will not take any of it back.
It was every word the fixed truth and perfect,

giving the flight attendant a blow job
        behind the curtain to the galley of the airplane at seventeen
on my way to London, where I fell in love for the umpteenth time,

blowing my heart into shrapnel.

Clipped wings stuffed in a duffle bag.
The methamphetamine boiling in its spoon
                beside the glass-mirrored waves of the Seine,
the geese in their flyway above our heads, so much longing.

Jouissance is this pleasure and pain.

I always loved male bonding, kissing the boys in Commander Salamanders,
their bloody noses slick against my cheek after the fights on M Street.

I still would do anything for you, ignite, shatter.
Strangle me.

I'll be some other man's winter skin, some other man's memory of war.
I still have so much to say to you, so much to tell.

Meet me there, stranger, behind the flags of sedition.

Sing your hymn, the footprints of your combat boots
                                where I would follow,
going down on you,

dig up the roots,

and find the nymphalidea, scatter of red spots on their black wings
Proboscis licking salt from the mud,

and a colony of leeches beneath the rocks, blood still pooled in their delicate
                                                                    cups.

American Ready Cut System Houses

Your postcard said, *Nothing like a little disaster to sort things out.*

Blueprints, sketches, such perfect houses in the photograph on the front,
all the lines true and in harmony. I took it with me like a paper charm,

searching for home, hit the road, looking for the exact spot
of my birthright, down the rustling path of thistles and nettles,

under a leaden sky, in the place where God once lifted

the home by its hair, nothing left but the kitchen and the bathtub
where we all hid. The supper table

picked up and carried to the county over and laid so gently down.

When I saw you last in the bar in Brooklyn, you told me to sing.
But I couldn't even speak. I laid my head in your lap,

drunk at two am and felt your hand resting across my back, reluctant,
unsure of what I wanted, but knowing

it was a want too much for anyone to give in to, a halter
broke, some rip.

The skeletons of the trees are coming back to life now, sap like stars
risen again. Most anything torn can be mended. No real

permanent damage. The land where the house was goes back
to the plum-colored dusk, hooks and hoods of the hawks

perching in the hemlocks, clouds and mounds of nebulae in the pitch night.

Frank Lloyd Wright said, *Nature will never fail you*, though I suppose it
                                                              depends
on what you mean by *fail*. It'll kill you for sure, Great Revelator.

You can hear the wilderness ad libbing its prayers in the whippoorwill and
the cypress,
in the percussion and boom of bittern in the bulrushes.

Dead is the mandible, alive the song, wrote Nabokov.

The bones of our houses, the house of our bones
dropped in a sudden blur of wind and wings,

but our voices still throb and palpitate somewhere, by some rapture,
in memory's ear, in the fluttering pages, behind the stars.

I have a song now I want to sing to you, but you're long gone.
When you said I'm here for you, was that a promise?

Overwhelm,

to bury or drown beneath a huge mass

Whelmen: *to turn upside down*

To turn over and over like a boat washed over and overset by a wave

To bring to ruin.

The end of one part of the world, a story that no longer has a witness.

But I'll sing it to myself. I'll sing it to the small moth,
the size of scarcely a word,

Ad libitum, according to my desire.

You Got to Pray to the Lord When You See Those Flying Saucers

Little Shepherd's creek is clogged, slow flow of black bile.
Blood red shots of bittersweet tangled on the barbed wire.
Bacchic orgy of snakes and Babel of birds.

This is the gospel of the woods.
The gospel of the caterpillar.
The gospel of the ground squirrel skips a blue streak through the dead leaves.
The gospel of the bloodroot and the jack in the pulpit.
Do you know the needs of your beasts, Lord?
Do you know?

The womb forgets. We are sweet to the worm.

Only humans know affliction. We are creatures of affliction.
Who we are to our core.

Open our inner ears.

I found a fox's den dug out of a scarp, roots like hag's hair.
Hole big enough to slide in feet first.

My grandmother heard voices in the radio antenna, copied
Bible verses in a frantic hand, letters scented with mothballs.

She said, *Your father loves you.* I never wrote back

and one day the letters stopped.

Let the waters teem with swarms of creatures that have a living soul.

My grandfather on my father's side invented AstroTurf.

He taught the ladies in Sunday school about the gospel

$$\text{written in the zodiac.}$$

Gospel of Venus who was Mary
Gospel of Trees clapping their hands in the forest of Andromeda.

When I left my father's house I came to the place where the girls were found:
Pink teeth, indicate possible violence, quick oxidation of hemoglobin
$\qquad\qquad\qquad\qquad\qquad$ *or possible strangulation*
remains found near water, no obvious taste of salt.

That's what they said: *no obvious taste.* What I want to know is
who tasted?
$\qquad\qquad$ *Lacrimae rerum*: the tears in things.

I once walked this trail with my Amish friend.
She pointed out the pennyroyal, abortifacient.
And on the cold rock of the talus slopes,
wolfbane, hunched in its monk's hood, deadly blue blooms.

All up and down the neighborhood
voices are calling from their windows—
They know everything about me.
They are drawing names.
They have a list and video surveillance.
There will be a midnight knock at the door.
Alert Today. Alive Tomorrow.

I sit out in winter smoking Camel Lights in the dead garden,
the brittle stalks of hollyhocks and sunflowers,
sky like mottled skin, blush and decomposing blue.

The stars look like spaceships. They come in low,
spotlight on me, my breasts cupped in my hands.

And I heard the beasts saying come and see come and see.

The Pond

The Mennonite girl hugged a basket to her body,
clutch of white turkey eggs.
Down by the drained pond they surrounded the drowned boy
with yellow caution tape.

Grief knocked its beak against its humble little shell.

The neighbor with a missile mounted in his front yard
came over and ushered her into the house.

The white blossoms of the cherry tree
flew in through the open window
and skittered across the wooden floorboards.

Copy: all, the image of God.
Same childlike impulse to blow the breath into clay.
Same breathless calamity.

Eat

In the dark of your bed, I am falling.
I'm your jackstone, your whetstone.
I'll be supine, like a fallen tree,
polished to mother of pearl.

Go back to Virginia.
Go down under the earth, where the soldiers
lie tangled together in their roots.

Go back to Virginia.
Go down by the river, where the boys of summer
undo their belts. I'll be waiting there for you.

Put your palm in my side like the rock
where the worms carve their trace.
Going down on you,
going down on me.

I want to see you bleed.

I'm sawn in half, girl in a box.
Split me apart and divide.
Rusty dress, the color of clots.

Gusts in the rushes on the edge of the creek,
war long passed, but the ghosts
of the little boats the soldiers sent
from shore to shore still float in the mist

bearing gifts for the other, for the stranger:

whisky in a flask, postcards and ephemera, a book.

My fingers read the braille
of the dead, their messages
rolled like scrolls into glass bottles,

letters to someone on the other side.

I'm calling to you from Chatham's hill.
I'm building a pontoon through the battery fire
in the gloaming.

War never ends, just shifts its winds
and the arrow on the ouija points
to some other stranger's name,

illegible and incomprehensible
as the smeared note washed up on the shore.
I'll never know who you are.

The clouds come in *mezza voce.*
I'm the iris with the starry night shoved down her throat.
Is there anyway to reach you?

I'll sweet talk you,
yolk of my tongue.

There's blood on your neck from my lips.

There's honey on the orchid
twenty-four hours before the bloom.
I'll lure you, like that.

Between thought and expression lies a lifetime

Your language and lexicon, like a silencer.
What makes us love what crushes us?

At the edge of arousal, anticipation of the fall,
the self at its terminus between your legs.

I'll be your reckoning, Oh
be mine. Oh Virginia, come inside.

Dear Apocalypse

I wanted to make something to cover your body,
so I made you a quilt, Tree of Life.
The back of the needle pierced my finger
and it bled on the binding.

You sent me a letter and called it a reliquary.
I know you think you're always dying, just like me.
We are brothers like that, one man in the field
and the other suddenly gone. Only I'm a woman

who wanted to be a man, loved male bonding,
John the Beloved, head in Jesus' lap.
When I lay my head on your pelvis, you start to shake.

I am sending you a spell from a pharmacia in L.A.,
Your end of the world, a coyote tooth
to keep the police away.

I don't believe in magic but I do.
I love the apocalypse in you.

Your handwriting on the envelope,
and the typed print and paper and Polaroids
you sent: image, medium, trace. Let us
be the question. Answers that miswandered,

Fidelity is the virtue of memory
and memory itself is a virtue, said Camus.

Soon, Soon.

Blow-Up

The postcard you sent of the bombed cafe in Lerouville, 1945
arrived at my studio on the night of the Paris bombings, 2015.
It was an accident, a fluke or fate. I could never have predicted

the future. *I can show you, when you come, the revolutionary places,*
you said. But we'll start small, go down to Gleason's gym
and watch the boys' sparring turn into real fights. Spray paint

a glass condo. You said, *Sometimes I like to go to Whole Foods*
In Tribeca and crush all the cookies in their packages
So the rich children will cry. I want to change the world,

make some disaster one day at a time. In the Polaroid you sent, I see
your hands grasping the camera. We don't know each other
but I could not resist the photographic image.

Accidents happen
and it may be more beautiful than what we intended.

There are things the mind already knows, said Rauschenberg,
painting his talismans.

Tip your head back, show me your throat.

Night coming down like a truck, fits of city lights on the windshield
like shards in your hair. All you've ever known
is this self alone, how much it wants, *hope without issue.*

Newsreel footage from a century ago,
flickering on the screen. Some dead in a pit
and you don't know their names, just a jolt of recognition,
but what is it you recognize? The dead?
The one who aims?

Nobody plays boxing, coach said.
Nobody plays this life and this living, either. A comet
flashing by above our tilted heads

as we lay on a blanket in the field of cut clover
necks milky white and slit with moonlight.

I was a fugitive, falling in love with you.
That night I told you the story
of my stepfather searching for my mother
through the streets of Fredericksburg
so he could kill her, maybe.

             The Virginia Line passed by the railroad houses

at the bottom of Lee's Hill, its mound of dead like a ziggurat.

He called me on the telephone at three am,
an old rotary with its heavy receiver like a weight in the hook of my hand
cradled to my ear, *You slut, you're a slut just like your mother.*

In your letter you wrote, *None of this is your fault.*

When I met you, it was all of a sudden and I was hit, unexpected.
I stopped eating and I wanted to die. Nabokov called it *toska.*
A heart-sickness.

        And while I laid there on my bed in the sheets, one hand on my clit,

the other inside of myself, a conflagration,

I imagined I was naked under the sky,
wind hot and smelling of cut wheat, the sifting of chaff.

Already I become this vision, I am becoming this vision every day.

In Memoriam

Those woods, my basilica, water in the spring, Holy. The color of
membranes, of abalone.

Wickerwork of birches surrounding us
        and the creak of branches, some reckoning music,
a counting down to that cross sighted, cross haired point,
           final ticking silence, we bow our heads to.

Encircled by that congregation of trees,
        feet half sunk in the mud
truing an invisible instrument in my body,
          finding its balance,
X it out, level, plumb.

While the constellations turned and my heart plowed
          this acreage. Drive it hard. Drive it in,

like the body of some fallen angel you press against,
        hands crushing a breast,

and thrust.

Karaoke

We drove up to Brooklyn from Virginia in the back of a flatbed,
our heads between each others legs. I'm not going to hide this desire.

Watch me, *all my stars as big as holes in my arms.* I'm this lovely child
turned girl with gun in my hand, now, Oh sugar, Oh delinquent,

I'll be that fist and punch
blood like red tulle spilling out of my mouth, your masochist.

Millions of red and green lights glittered in the ceiling of Hank's Saloon,
throbbed like capillaries, jewel-colored clots.

And my red velvet slippers were soaked in piss from the bathroom
where me met face to face, your pupils like the percussion of a self blacking out

and finding itself again in light, misspelled on a blank page,
a beauty that infuriates, like a disaster, like an accident.

The band played *I wanna be your dog.*

The crowd pulled you deeper in, the bodies of strangers
floating through you like peat smoke and all I could see
was the sheet lightning on your sleeves and in your hair.

I leaned against Big Buck Hunter and lifted my hands above my head
like I was *wanted*, pinned in the gun's sight, legs spread, split fig.

A slug in the shoulder,
a slug over the breast bone like a song that destroys the passerby
with its noise and thrust

opening its mouth wide.
The glory-hole of a song like a storm,
                                        sucking me off.

Scapegoat

You can pray a hedge of protection

but it won't be wide enough for where I go.

You stole my goat

      and sliced its belly open.

I told you not to.

      You said you were a liar and a thief.

I said don't be a murderer, too.

Its guts unraptured, unspooled
      and glistening with blood.

It was the final straw. I wore a dress of flies,
      buzzing up your nostrils

and fled out into the plain.

I remembered as I went, the way it used to be, I

was just a dwarf star, always undressing.

Out here there are no names for things.

No bluebells or cardinal flowers.

No palindrome epitaphs on the Mennonite graves.

No mountains ringed in honeycolored smoke.

No names of manacled saints who hack themselves into chunks.

No four part a cappella song compressing the little boy's chest.

No old woman tying knots with red thread.

All of it is lost. All charms and amulets, seals and spells.

And I become nothing, the ghost of my head cradled in the cup of your pelvis.

Like exhaled breath, I am forgotten already.

Love Letter

I watched the fights for years in reverence, you said.
The stagger and collapse and heap.

                              Was it you who went down, or me?

My own notoriety grew its teeth in your mouth,
                              tiny orchids you find in the dark,

some obscenity, some violence budding in the deep woods and the swamp.

Share anything with me, you said. But you took it back.

I was the hard shove. I straddled your mouth.
I could stiffen you in two heats.

Don't you want to rub spit on your hands and press your wet fingers in?

Resist the temptation, you said, *to destroy.*

Look, the architecture and anatomy you thought
                              you knew by heart has just fractured,

maybe it's walking like trees walking,
                    maybe the corpse has dropped its garments and turned to air.

I'm getting exhilarated just writing about it, you said.

I have to tell you my Gibby Haynes story.

                              I promise I'm not stalking you.
My chest like a Cornell box.

My skin in bandages.

                              I use my hair to sweep the room.

Your first love was Camus?

Still thinking of you, you said.

                                             Troubled, troubled, in our hearts.

Are you still here?
I'm here for you, you said.

                        Boy on the rocks in the middle of the Rappahannock,
unzip your jeans.

The Play

We were in the Cherry Orchard
sitting on the stage, the actors

close enough to touch, and we touched.
Pool table behind us, double red

in the middle pocket. Hold my tongue,
hold my tongue. Bookcase to the left, beloved.

It smells like patchouli in here! Your knees
pressed against mine, Chekov open

between my legs, and I could hear
the light gasps of your breath

and the quiet laugh down in your throat
like small fish, swimming in a brook.

When Lopakhin kissed Varvara,
when he grabbed her face with his fist

and forced her, I heard the string in your body
and the string in mine tighten like an orchestra,

tuning up. I know you were watching me,
though you looked at them. You know

I was watching you, though I closed my eyes
tight.

One Last Thing

I have to tell you the story of the night you didn't want to see me
and I was alone. Muhammad Ali died and all I wanted was to tell you
what you already knew, like words I took right out of your mouth,
how love can get up on the count of nine. I spent the night
in a room I rented from a stranger. Fluorescent lights buzzed
in the halls of the old asylum, 2 am. An elevator with a cage door,
clack of cables in the shaft. All of a sudden I was back
in the south of France, Nimes, the landlord chewing on his cigar.
I smelled like sex, a rough, blood-stained parchment, smudged
with fingerprints. The crowd roared in the arena, Feria de Pentecôte,
brass bands marched through the streets, girls in swirling flamenco skirts,
and small boys whipped the bulls with straps, running for cover.
I followed them down to the Corrida to watch, the only one
who remembers, longing so much to tell you, make you my witness.
On the sixth floor of the Brooklyn apartment, a man stood
in the doorway, lamplight behind his body darkening him into shadow,
calling out my name. I was afraid, suddenly, all of it so familiar,
because I had been raped before and it felt familiar, like a story
I know by heart. In my Brooklyn bed, I straddled the photographs
of you spread out on the sheets and wept for what gets ripped inside us,
how we pull or push too hard, go too deep in until suddenly someone
you want to love or someone you wish would love you back is gone.
Maybe you broke them, some bone fractured, and you feel ashamed
at your own violence, *Come in close and don't stop hitting,* until
you snap to, and it dawns on you that this is not the ring, not the place
to throw your punches, but by then it's too late, blood everywhere
and no one cheering. I stayed afraid half the night, fear balled like a t-shirt
stuffed in my mouth, a clog, a clot. What is the name of this song I sing
over and over like a gag? No words left, just a hum deep in the throat
like moan. I cross the threshold, back again over the bloody carpet
where he pressed my head against the floor, tightening a vice, ears sticky
with plasma. Go back now. Follow the trail of blood behind the bull
hooked and dragged out by horses. Mediterranean sun beat down, so hot
on my hair, your hand caught in the tangled strands of light. A shadow
behind the door calls my name and I go in. But where were you
when I was afraid? Where did you go? You made promises,
I'm here for you and *share anything with me,* what words are.

What's said should mean something like bond, like scar on your skin,
a rare handwritten note, messages tattooed on tobacco papers, rolled
and smoked, inhaled into your lungs. I told you everything, all the details
of my own assault. But I'm one to talk, saying one thing and doing another,
so many vows I just can't keep. We are cut from the same fragile cloth,
a thin garment of language. When you kissed me on the side of my face,
did that mean you were giving me your blessing, just to be in your life,
which somehow translated for me into being alive? All my flesh measured
in your *no* or *yes*. I hoped it wasn't goodbye. I can still feel your five o'clock
shadow on my cheek and under my palm when we were in Hank's Saloon
and I drew your ear down to my mouth with my hand on the side of your face,
so I could tell you something, and I kept thinking of more things to say.
Muhammad Ali is dead. I'm not trying to seduce you, I'm just telling you
things I want to remember forever about being alive, the way the blood
unspooled out from the wound and pissed its ribbons on the sand,
the way the knives shuddered with every heartbeat and thump of that dying
                                                                    beast.
The sticky sweetness of life matted in its fur. I have no motive or intention.
                                                                    You
had to pry me out by my hair. All I wanted was to sit and listen to you tell me
something, because whatever you had to say would be something new
and I'd rush right down to the arena and write a poem and plunge my
                                                            bandolero
through the heart of it. Put my dress back over my head,
write a quick note to me in the morning and leave it on the bed, I know
                                                            exactly
what I want you to write, tell me you'll see me soon, tonight—
Tell me you'll meet me ringside at the fight.

Notes

Some of the poems in this book include quotations from other sources:

"Glass Jaw"
"The past is connected to the present like a man's arm to his shoulder"
    from *The Sweet Science*, A.J. Liebling (North Point Press, 2004)

"Hazel Run"
    David Bowie, of course.

"Catherine's Furnace"
"Nabokov said nature was a form of magic, like art."
    from *Nabokov's Butterflies, Boyd, Brian and Pyle*, Robert Michael
    (Beacon Press, Boston, 2000)

Proverbs 25:22

"Stitch"
"Performed pain is still pain"
    from *Grand Unified Theory of Female Pain*, Leslie Jamison (*Virginia
    Quarterly Review*, Spring 2014)

"K.O"
"Yesterday I was lying, but today I am telling the truth."
    Bob Arum on Sugar Ray Leonard:

"Gouge"
"One man said there are hundreds / of delicate articulated bones/ in the
human head. So don't let it get punched."
    from *The Sweet Science*, A.J. Liebling

"Julian Schnabel in His Studio on West 111th Street"
"Not being able to touch is sometimes as interesting as touching"
    from "Rivers and Tides" in "Andy Goldsworthy Working with Time"

"American Ready Cut System Houses"
"Your postcard said, Nothing like a little disaster to sort things out."
    from "Blow Up," Michelangelo Antonioni

"Dead is the mandible, alive the song, wrote Nabokov."
      from *Pale Fire*, Vladimir Nabokov (G.P. Putnam's Sons, 1962)
I am also indebted to Charles Wright, my first teacher, for a certain cadence
in this poem. I hear his voice in the poem's ear.

"Eat"
"I want to see you bleed."
      from "Welcome to the Jungle," Guns N' Roses

"Between thought and expression lies a lifetime"
      from "Some Kind of Love," Velvet Underground

"What makes us love what crushes us?"
      from "The Myth of Sisyphus," Albert Camus

"Karaoke"
"Watch me, all my stars as big as holes in my arms. I'm this lovely child/
turned girl with gun in my hand"—Patti Smith

Acknowledgments

"Catherine's Furnace," "Flash," "Hazel Run," "The Quarry," "XXX," and "You Got to Pray to the Lord When You See Those Flying Saucers" originally appeared in *The Missouri Review*.

"One Last Thing" originally appeared in *Night Jar Review*.

I would like to thank Todd Smith and my family, Olivia, Owen, and Elliot; Tom Simpson, Chris Kasper, and Ben Apatoff for letters and correspondence, encouragement, care, and kindness; the support of my friends in Bosnia-Herzegovina and Fredericksburg, Virginia; my teachers, Charles Wright, Mark Doty, Rita Dove, Greg Orr, Marvin Bell; The Lexi Rudnitsky Poetry Project, Persea Books; and xo's and hugs to my editor Gabriel Fried for his guidance and support.

About the Lexi Rudnitsky Editor's Choice Award

The Lexi Rudnitsky Editor's Choice Award is given annually to a poetry collection by a writer who has published at least once previous book of poems. Along with the Lexi Rudnitsky First Book Prize in Poetry, it is a collaboration of Persea Books and the Lexi Rudnitsky Poetry Project. Entry guidelines for both awards are available on Persea's website (www.perseabooks.com).

Lexi Rudnitsky (1972–2005) grew up outside of Boston, and studied at Brown University and Columbia University. Her own poems exhibit both a playful love of language and a fierce conscience. Her writing appeared in *The Antioch Review, Columbia: A Journal of Literature and Art, The Nation, The New Yorker, The Paris Review, Pequod,* and *The Western Humanities Review.* In 2004, she won the Milton Kessler Memorial Prize for Poetry from *Harpur Palate.*

Lexi died suddenly in 2005, just months after the birth of her first child and the acceptance for publication of her first book of poems, *A Doorless Knocking into Night* (Mid-List Press, 2006). The Lexi Rudnitsky book prizes were created to memorialize her by promoting the type of poet and poetry in which she so spiritedly believed.

Previous winners of the Lexi Rudnitsky Editor's Choice Award

2015	Shane McCrae	*The Animal Too Big to Kill*
2014	Caki Wilkinson	*The Wynona Stone Poems*
2013	Michael White	*Vermeer in Hell*
2012	Mitchell L. H. Douglas	*blak al-febet*
2011	Amy Newman	*Dear Editor*